This book is for O

Text and illustrations copyright © 2000 by Chris Raschka.
For information address Hyperion Books for Children,
114 Fifth Avenue, New York, New York 10011-5690.

First Edition
1 3 5 7 9 10 8 6 4 2
Printed in Singapore.

Library of Congress Cataloging-in-Publication Data
Raschka, Christopher.
Wormy Worm / by Chris Raschka. —1st ed.
p. cm.— (Thingy things)
Summary: As Wormy Worm wiggles and woggles, it is hard to tell
which end is front and which end is back.
ISBN 0-7868-0582-X (trade)
[1. Worms—Fiction.] I. Title II. Series: Raschka, Christopher.
Thingy things.
PZ7.R18148Wo   2000
[E]--dc21   99-39587

Visit www.hyperionchildrensbooks.com,
part of the GO Network

THINGY THINGS
Wormy Worm

Chris Raschka

HYPERION BOOKS FOR CHILDREN
NEW YORK

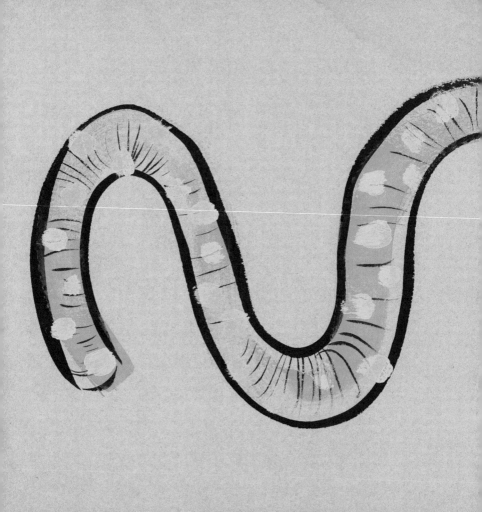

Wormy Worm wiggles.

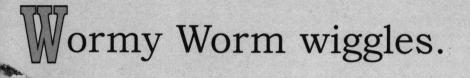

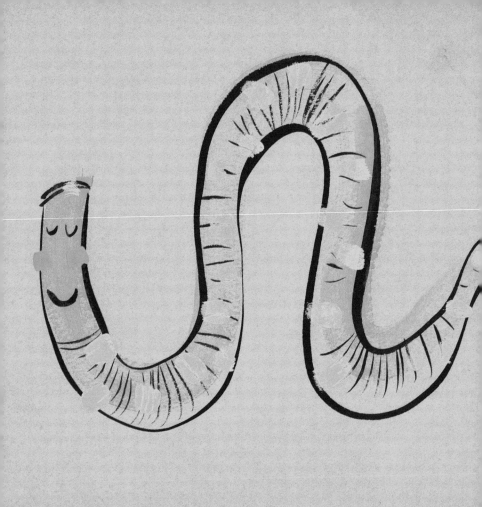

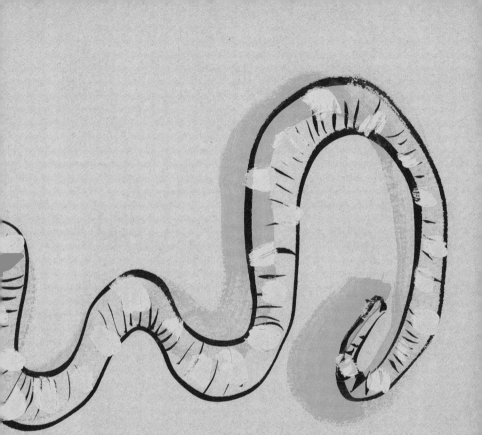

He wiggles and woggles.

Ha ha ha

Hee hee hee

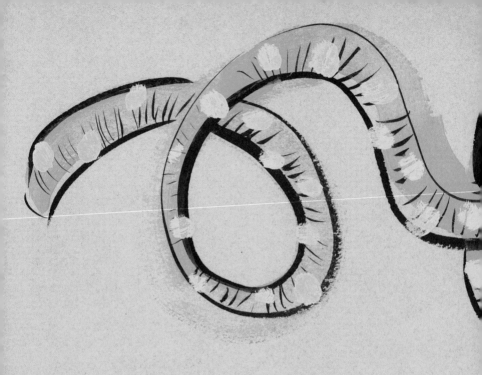

Ho ho ho

Hee hee ha

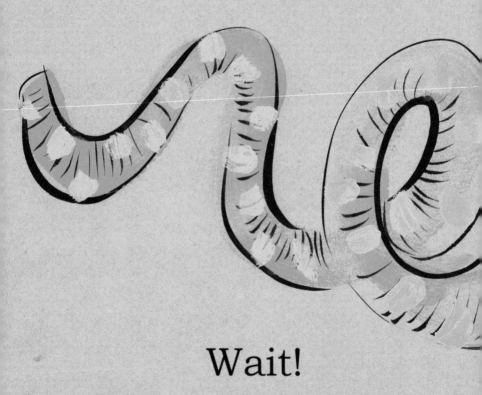

Wait!

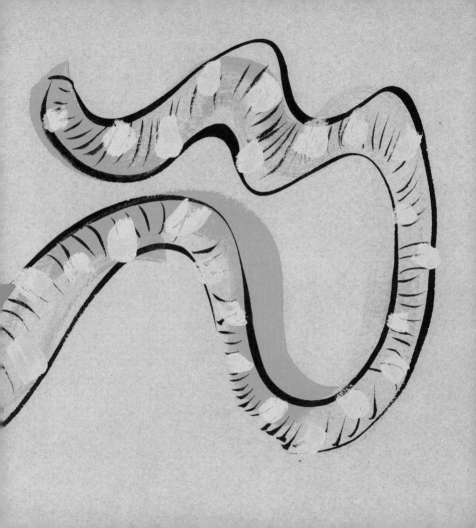

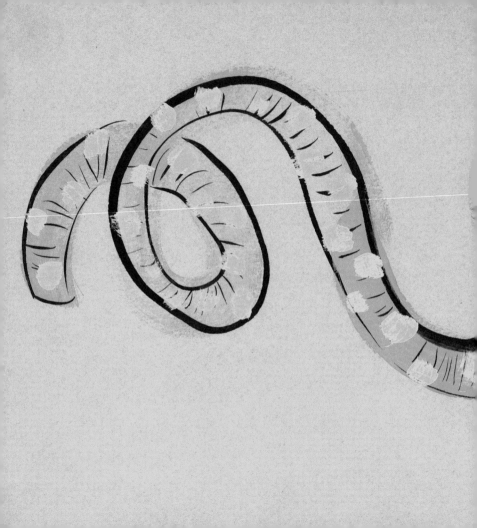

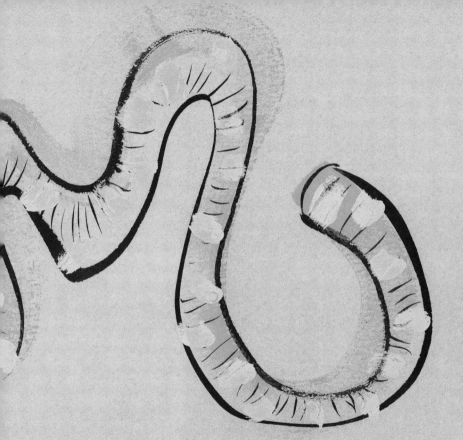

Which end is front?

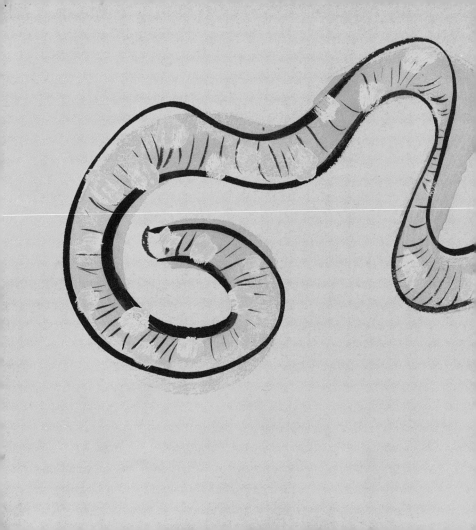

Which end is back?

Wormy Worm!